Dear mouse friends,
Welcome to the world of

Geronimo Stilton

THE RODENT'S GAZETTE
EDITORIAL STAFF

Geronimo Stilton
A learned and brainy
mouse; editor of
The Rodent's Gazette

Thea Stilton
Geronimo's sister and
special correspondent at
The Rodent's Gazette

   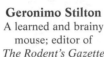 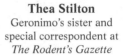

Trap Stilton
An awful joker;
Geronimo's cousin and
owner of the store
Cheap Junk for Less

Benjamin Stilton
A sweet and loving
nine-year-old mouse;
Geronimo's favorite
nephew

Geronimo Stilton

THE CHEESE EXPERIMENT

Scholastic Inc.

Published by Scholastic Inc., *Publishers since 1920*, 557 Broadway, New York, NY 10012. SCHOLASTIC and associated logos are trademarks and/or registered trademarks of Scholastic Inc.

Stilton is the name of a famous English cheese. It is a registered trademark of the Stilton Cheese Makers' Association. For more information, go to www.stiltoncheese.com.

This book is a work of fiction. Names, characters, places, and incidents are either the product of the author's imagination or are used fictitiously, and any resemblance to actual persons, living or dead, business establishments, events, or locales is entirely coincidental.

ISBN 978-0-545-87252-2

Text by Geronimo Stilton
Original title *Lo strano caso dei brufoli blu*
Cover by Giuseppe Ferrario (design) and Giulia Zaffaroni (color)
Illustrations by Andrea De Negri (design) and Valentina Grassini (color)
Graphics by Marta Lorini

Special thanks to Shannon Penney
Translated by Lidia Morson Tramontozzi
Interior design by Kay Petronio

10 9 8 7 6 5 4 3 2 1   16 17 18 19 20

Printed in the U.S.A.   40
First printing 2016

A SUPER-SPECIAL DAY

One cool and peaceful Monday in late **SEPTEMBER**, I woke up early, stretched my paws over my head, and got ready for a *SUPER-SPECIAL* day . . .

Brush, brush!

I BRUSHED MY TEETH WITH CHEESEMINT TOOTHPASTE. YUM!

OOPS, I'm sorry — I forgot to introduce myself! My name is Stilton, *Geronimo Stilton*. I'm the editor of *The Rodent's Gazette*, the most famouse newspaper on Mouse Island.

My job keeps me busy, but that morning I was headed to my nephew Benjamin's school for the opening of their new **science labs**. I was supposed to give a speech! I wanted to look sophisticated for FOUR REASONS:

I COMBED MY FUR WITH SLEEKFUR . . .

I PUT ON MY FRESHLY PRESSED SUIT . . .

1) To make my little nephew proud.

2) Because the school principal is a good **friend** of mine.

3) Because I **knew** that Dr. Margo Bitmouse — otherwise known as **Doc** — would be there. She's a marvemousely smart and beautiful rodent!

4) Because my grandfather had called and hollered, "**GRANDSON!** Did you comb your whiskers? Did you write a good speech? Don't be a **cheesebrain**. The reputation of

I PUT ON A RED SILK TIE. VERY FANCY!

I SPRAYED MYSELF WITH A HINT OF PARMESAN COLOGNE.

The Rodent's Gazette is at stake!"

So I took a little longer than usual to make sure I looked *mouserific*. Finally, I checked myself in the **mirror** one last time and grinned. Not bad!

I hailed a **TAXI** and headed to Benjamin's school. On the ride, I went over the speech in my head — but the closer we got to the school, the more my tail *trembled* and my

whiskers wobbled! Holey cheese, I was a **WRECK**!

The taxi driver was a rodent around Grandfather William's age. He was large and had a thick gray handlebar **MUSTACHE**. He kept glancing at me in the rearview mirror.

At a **RED LIGHT**, he turned to face me. "Aren't you Geronimo Stilton? The

Yes, that's me!

publisher of *The Rodent's Gazette*?"

I nodded. "Yes, that's me!"

"Mr. Stilton, your snout is as white as a slice of MOZZARELLA cheese!" he said, looking worried. "Are you feeling okay? Are you getting carsick? There's a special SICKNESS BAG under the seat — I always keep a few handy for weak-stomached rodents like you."

I held up a paw and tried to reassure him. "Oh, it's not car sickness. I promise. I'm just nervous! When I get to the school, I have to:

1) walk a red carpet in front of hundreds of rodents (without tripping!),

2) give a **SPEECH** in front of hundreds of rodents and TV reporters (without forgetting what to say!), and

3) cut the inaugural ribbon for the new science labs (without snipping my paw!)."

The cabdriver raised an eyebrow and muttered, "Mr. Stilton, I assumed you were a brilliant, carefree mouse, like your grandfather **WILLIAM SHORTPAWS**! I had the pleasure of driving him around in my cab quite often in the old days."

Cheese and crackers! I tried to **justify** myself.

"Well, usually . . . I mean, sometimes . . .

actually . . . I'm more or less an easygoing mouse. But today I have to give a speech, and I'm so worried about it that my **fur** is standing on end! Excuse me . . ."

I buried my snout in the **pages** of my speech.

"**Humph**, they don't make journalists the way they used to," the cabdriver grumbled. "Your grandfather William was a real journalist — not a **Cheddarhead** like you!"

By now we had arrived at New Mouse City's elementary school, the same school I went to as a mouseling. As I climbed out of the taxi, I noticed something weird. There were little **BLUE CLOUDS** hovering in the air outside the school, and it **stunk** of garlic!

Cheese niblets,

HOW STRANGE!

A Calm, Brilliant, Confident Mouse?

Even though I was more **NERVOUS** than a mouse in a room full of cats, the morning went well. I climbed the school steps without tripping and greeted my friend the principal with a polite KISS ON THE PAW.

"You're such a gentlemouse, Geronimo!" she squeaked.

Here I am! Geronimo!

Smack!

I didn't freeze when I gave my **speech**, even though hundreds of reporters were watching and filming me for all the TV stations on Mouse Island. I didn't get tongue-tied even once — a record for a shy mouse like me!

And when I **CUT** the yellow ribbon to open the new ultra-modern science labs, I didn't nick my **Paws**, snip off any whiskers, or get tangled up in the ribbon. Slimy Swiss cheese, it was a **miracle**!

Was I finally becoming a calm, brilliant, and **CONFIDENT** rodent?

I scurried into the new science labs, feeling marvemouse.

When the principal began showing us the new **lab** equipment, I stood up straight and held my snout high in the air, just like a mouse who was calm, brilliant, and confident . . . but I didn't pay attention to the freshly waxed floor!

Proudly, I approached the principal to compliment her. "This lab is absolutely a state-of-the-art —"

I'm so cool!

Yiiiikes!

Science Lab

SWISSHHH

I didn't have time to finish before I slipped on the waxed floor! After doing a **double-twisted** death-defying **somersault**, I ended up with my snout in the garbage can.

So much for being a calm, brilliant, confident mouse . . .

! ! . SQUEAK! ! ! !
! I FELT LIKE SUCH
! A CHEESEBRAIN! !

What a cheesebrain!

Ohhhh . . .

Ouch! Ouch!

I pulled my head out of the garbage can and saw the principal staring at me with a *funny* look on her snout. My face turned as **RED** as the tomato sauce on a double-cheese pizza! I tried to crack a joke.

"I know it looks like I *slipped*, but, um, I was just making sure the floor was perfectly smooth!"

The principal raised an eyebrow. "What about *diving* into the garbage can?"

Looking down at my paws, I muttered, "I was, uh, checking to see if it was empty . . ."

SQUEAK! I FELT LIKE SUCH A CHEESEBRAIN!

Squeak!

She burst out *laughing*. "Geronimo, you haven't changed a whisker since we were in elementary school!"

And then — rat-munching rattlesnakes! — she kissed me lightly on the tip of my snout. Now I was red from the ends of my ears to the tip of my tail!

At that moment, I noticed something strange. There was an enormouse ⓑⓛⓤⓔ ⓢⓟⓞⓣ on the principal's snout!

Huh?

A blue spot!

MOLDY MOZZARELLA — A BLUE SPOT!

Rotten rats' teeth! An ugly blue spot had popped up on my friend's snout! It was so **ENORMOUSE** and so **blue** that I couldn't stop staring at it.

Tugging on her whiskers nervously, she asked, "Why are you staring at my snout?"

I didn't want to offend her, so I muttered, "Oh, I was just looking at your beautiful blue eyes . . ."

"My eyes aren't blue," she said slowly. "They're **BLACK**!"

Whoops.

She opened her purse, pulled out a mirror, and squeaked, "Thundering cat tails — what is that blue spot?" The principal looked like she was about to faint from shock.

A second later, I heard a loud squeak from another mouse.

"Moldy mozzarella — a blue spot!"

Then I heard another squeak . . . and another . . . and another!

"Rancid ricotta — a blue spot!"

For the love of cheese, what was happening?

Just then I felt an **itch** on my snout. Did I have a blue spot, too? While everyone headed off to grab refreshments, I scampered to the **BATHROOM** . . .

Phew — I was safe! No b l u e

SPOTS! I headed back to the lab, but I couldn't help thinking that this whole thing was awfully STRANGE.

And that's when I ran into my sister, Thea — and Doc! Doc is a tough, energetic, intelligent, and very beautiful rodent.

DOC

She's fabumouse! But every time I see her, I always get my tail in a twist and end up looking like a complete cheesebrain!

I was just hoping she hadn't seen my somersault — the one that ended with a dive into the garbage can. Maybe she had been looking the other way . . .

Doc PINCHED my cheeks and squeaked, "Nice job, my little cheese puff — you gave a marvemouse speech. And congrats on that tumble, too!" She winked.

Peering at my paws, I headed toward the refreshments with my †A!L between my legs. But when I got there, I forgot all about my embarrassment . . . because most of the rodents near me were covered with 𝕓𝕝𝕦𝕖 𝕤𝕡𝕠𝕥𝕤!

I scampered over to the principal and whispered, "Um, these blue spots **worry** me!"

I lowered my voice even further. "Should we send everyone home? They could be **CONTAGIOUS**..."

"You're right, Geronimo," she said, nodding her snout seriously.

She walked up to the MICROPHONE and announced, "Dear rodent friends, thank you for coming on this special day! Unfortunately, we have to bring the FESTIVITIES to an end. It was wonderful seeing all of you. Thank you, and good-bye!"

An Enormouse Banana Ice Cream Cone

I took Benjamin's paw and headed out of the school. As we walked, he squeaked happily, "Uncle G, your speech was awesome!"

Next to him, **Bugsy Wugsy** chuckled. "The best part, though, was the surprise ending when you **dove** into the garbage can!"

I pretended I hadn't heard her because Doc had just walked out of the school. She **pinched** me on the cheek again and said, "Nice job, my little cheese puff! The principal told me it was your idea to send everyone home. You're right — those blue spots do seem contagious. Maybe you're not a **HOPELESS CHEDDARHEAD** after all . . ."

Flustered, I blurted, "Oh, compliment for the thanks. I mean, thanks for the compliment, even if I'm not really, totally, completely sure that what you said was a compliment, because I have a feeling you just said I'm a **HOPELESS CHEDDARHEAD** . . . but I always hope that I **DON'T** look like a cheddarhead! Anyway, thanks!"

With that, Doc walked away, chuckling to herself.

SQUEAK! I FELT LIKE SUCH A CHEESEBRAIN!

Maybe you're not a hopeless cheddarhead!

Um . . .

I wanted to tear out my whiskers — but I couldn't let Benjamin and Bugsy see my frustration! So I tried not to let my fur get ruffled. Instead, I said, "How about some **ice cream**?"

"Yes! Fabumouse!" Bugsy and Benjamin squeaked excitedly.

We went to the Icy Rat, which has the best ice cream in New Mouse City. We sat down at a small table and each ordered the house specialty: **seven flavors of yum.**

It was whisker-licking-good! I had just started on the second **layer** of my ice cream — mascarpone and mint — when I heard a voice whisper, "Hey you! Pssst!"

Holey cheese — I thought

I recognized that voice! I turned around but didn't see anyone. So I shrugged, picked up my spoon, and dug into the ice cream again.

"Hey you! Pssst! Pssst! I'm talking to you!"

I turned again, but the only thing I saw was an enormouse plastic banana-flavored ICE CREAM cone.

STRANGE!

I was about to take another bite of ice cream when someone

smacked me on the back so hard that I ended up snout-deep in my bowl. "Geronimo, I've called you **three times** now!"

Crusty cat litter! After I wiped the mascarpone-mint ice cream out of my eyes, I turned around for the third time.

I saw a familiar snout with huge **teeth** pop out of the plastic banana-flavored ice cream cone.

"Pssst, it's me — Hercule Poirat! Do you like my **DiSGUiSE**?"

I've called you three times!

"Hercule?" I whispered in surprise. "What are you doing here?"

"I'm investigating," he explained. "I want you to keep your eyes wide open. There's a **MYSTERY** apaw, Geronimo, and I need you to help me solve it!"

HERCULE POIRAT is a famous private detective and one of my good friends. He's always trying to get me involved in his crazy investigations!

Hercule? What are you doing here?

I couldn't help being intrigued. "What kind of **MYSTERY** is it this time?"

"I don't know **YET**," Hercule said, lowering his voice to a whisper. "But stay

HERCULE POIRAT

First Name: Hercule

Last Name: Poirat

Who He Is:
Geronimo's friend
since preschool. He's
been playing pranks
on Geronimo since
they were tiny
mouselings!

Profession:
Private investigator.
He runs the Poirat Agency.

Hobbies: He has a real passion for jokes and
disguises. He loves to surprise Geronimo while
wearing different costumes.

His Dream: To fight evil!

His Battle Cry: "Have no fear, Hercule Poirat
is here!"

His Secret: He loves to eat bananas,
because he thinks they cure everything
from colds to calluses!

on your paws, keep your eyes wide open, and **BE ALERT**! Got it, Geronimo?"

I squeaked, "How can I **BE ALERT** if I don't even know what I'm supposed to be looking for?"

But Hercule had already **VANISHED**!

Bugsy and Benjamin hadn't noticed anything. They were too busy gobbling up their ice cream! When they got to the seventh layer — spicy Gorgonzola and chocolate with pistachios — they both squeaked for the seventh time, "Holey cheese, this is soooo good!"

When they finally looked up from their empty cups, they gaped at me with **FUNNY LOOKS** on their snouts. Then they both burst out laughing!

"You really liked your ice cream, huh, Uncle G?" Benjamin said with a giggle.

"It's all over you! You look like you did a SNOUTDIVE right into the bowl!"

! ! ! SQUEAK! ! ! I FELT LIKE SUCH A CHEESEBRAIN !

You liked it that much, huh?

You did a snoutdive!

News Flash!

I took Benjamin and Bugsy home, then scampered back to my house. Rancid ricotta, I was so sticky from the ice cream that an annoying swarm of *flies* had begun buzzing all around me! To get rid of them, I took a warm shower, **scrubbed my fur** with mozzarella-scented soap, and finished with a dusting of fresh cheese-scented powder.

Yum!

Once I was clean, I wandered into the kitchen for a snack. I made myself a **triple-decker** cheese sandwich, along with a huge mozzarella milkshake.

Yum!

I turned on the **TV** to watch the news and began nibbling on my SANDWICH. But what I heard the reporter say almost made me choke on my cheese!

"ALARMING news flash from New Mouse City, Mouse Island's capital," he began. "It seems that rodents there have been struck by a bizarre disease — a disease that is very contagious and produces strange blue spots! The best scientists in New Mouse City are currently looking into this bizarre phenomenon. Stay tuned to WRAT TV for the latest!"

Gulp!

I turned off the TV, gobbled down my food, and got DRESSED

faster than a rat with a cat on his tail. Then I called *The Rodent's Gazette* office. Everyone there sounded totally **rattled**!

Before I could **SQUEAK**, Priscilla Prettywhiskers shouted, "**BOSS!** Where are you? Did you hear about the blue spots? What do you want us to do?"

"Priscilla, *SHAKE A PAW* and get all the editors together for an emergency meeting!" I said.

I hung up and called Mayor Frederick

Fuzzypaws, one of my old friends. He cried, "*Geronimo!* I need your help to **REASSURE** New Mouse City's rodents about this blue spot breakout. I'm counting on you!"

The next rodent I called was Thea, who also shouted in my ear. "Geronimo! Did you hear the NEWS about the blue spots?"

"Of course I did!" I squeaked. "I need you to call all our friends and family except for Grandfather. Have them meet us at *The Rodent's Gazette* office in two shakes of a mouse's tail!"

I hung up and hightailed it

Boss!

Geronimo!

Did you hear the news?

to *The Rodent's Gazette*. Out on the street, I was struck squeakless. It looked like many rodents had already reacted to the **EMERGENCY** — and they'd taken matters into their own paws in all different ways!

First, a **strange** mouse wearing a **WET SUIT**, goggles, and a snorkel accidentally stepped on my tail.

Up here, the air is cleaner!

It's aluminum foil, to ward off germs!

Another was walking on Stilts — to breathe cleaner air, he said — and another had wrapped himself in aluminum foil. One rodent had even smeared herself with a concoction made of rotten Gorgonzola cheese. She was surrounded by a cloud of flies! Rats, what a smell!

Pinching my snout, I asked, "Escuze be. Why bid yu zbear yurzelf wid rodded

What's going on?

A ROTTEN GORGONZOLA CONCOCTION!

Corconzola?" (Translation: "Excuse me. Why did you smear yourself with rotten Gorgonzola?")

She answered, "Mr. Stilton, I thought it was obvious — the smell keeps the **germs** away! Know who told me? My furdresser's mother-in-law's friend's . . ."

But I stopped listening when I spotted Trap. He was wearing a deepwater **diver's**

What a smell!

helmet! He started talking to me, but with that **HELMET** over his snout, I couldn't hear a single word. I stared at his mouth, and after a while I figured out what he was saying by reading his **LIPS**.

"You'll catch the blue spots! NAH-NAH-NAH-NAH-NAH!" he singsonged. "I have this helmet, so I don't have to worry!"

AN ENORMOUSELY IMPORTANT CURE!

When I arrived at *The Rodent's Gazette*, the conference room was packed! We had to put a double row of chairs around the table so that everyone could fit.

EVERYONE was there — the staff of *The Rodent's Gazette*, plus ALL of my friends and relatives, including Grandfather William! Cheese and crackers! I had left instructions not to tell him about the meeting, but there he was in the front row.

Grandfather always manages to find out about everything. And when there's an EMERGENCY,

GRANDFATHER WILLIAM

he scampers back to *The Rodent's Gazette* and takes control!

As soon as he saw me, he squeaked, "There's no time to waste! The city is in chaos, and the ⓑⓛⓤⓔ ⓢⓟⓞⓣⓢ are popping up everywhere. Get your tail in gear!"

Trap jumped up and showed us a **sign** that he had written. It said, *Here's the solution: a good helmet. Ta-da!*

"Trap, I don't think that's going to work,"
I said, scratching my snout. "We can't live
with helmets over our snouts all the time.
We need to find a REAL SOLUTION!"

"Well said, Grandson! You do seem
somewhat intelligent when you try,"
Grandfather William said. "And because
I'm always a paw ahead of you, I've already
asked my friend *Professor Brainymouse*
to find the solution!"

Only then did I notice the **intelligent-
looking** rodent seated next to my
grandfather. He cleared his throat and
squeaked, "Rodents, diving helmets and
other do-it-yourself remedies don't work!
To *fight* this strange disease, we first
have to pinpoint exactly what it is. Once we
know that, then we find the CURE!"

Trap shrugged and held up another

Professor Brainymouse

Name: Professor Brainymouse
Eyes: Dark and sparkling
Height: Very tall
Residence: 103 Neuron Way, New Mouse City
Profession: Doctor and researcher (He has thirteen doctorate degrees!)
Distinguishing Features: He's always smiling.
His Secret: He's a vegetarian — he doesn't eat any meat.
His Motto: "Better to prevent than to cure!"

SIGN: *I'll never take off the helmet! You never know what could happen. I don't want to get sick!*

Moldy mozzarella, once my cousin gets a **furbrained** idea in his head, there's no stopping him!

"What about us?" asked **THEA**. "What can *The Rodent's Gazette* do?"

Professor Brainymouse smiled.

Here's a little list!

"YOU CAN DO A LOT! HERE'S A LITTLE LIST . . ."

I quickly read his list and announced, "No problem. We'll take care of getting the most **CRUCIAL INFORMATION** out to the citizens of New Mouse City!"

The professor got up and SQUEAKED, "Thank you! In the meantime, I'll scurry over to the laboratory and **START** on the Research immediately. Professor Von Volt, Doc, and a group of the best researchers in New Mouse City

HERE'S WHAT THE RODENT'S GAZETTE WILL DO:

1) KEEP RODENTS INFORMED BY PRINTING A SPECIAL EDITION OF THE RODENT'S GAZETTE DETAILING HOW EVERYONE SHOULD RESPOND TO THIS CRISIS.

2) RAISE FUNDS TO FINANCE THE RESEARCH.

3) WRITE, COPY, AND DISTRIBUTE FLYERS DETAILING KEY STEPS THAT ALL RODENTS SHOULD FOLLOW:

• ALWAYS WASH PAWS WITH SOAP AND WATER.

• EAT PLENTY OF FRUITS AND VEGETABLES TO STRENGTHEN THE IMMUNE SYSTEM.

• KEEP CALM AND CONTACT YOUR DOCTOR WITH QUESTIONS.

are **waiting** for me!"

As soon as I heard the name *Doc*, I blushed and stammered, "Er . . . I—I—I would be happy to go with you. So that I can . . . keep the readers up-to-date with the progress of my engage — I mean, the progress of the research!"

Professor Brainymouse *looked* at me like I had three snouts! He checked in my eyes, checked my pulse, took my blood pressure, and ordered me to open my mouth.

"Hmmm . . . WHITE eyeballs, high blood pressure, red ears, **pink** cheeks, **wobbly** legs, tongue-tied. There's no doubt! It's a bad case of —".

Rancid ricotta! I quickly interrupted him.

"Professor, tell me the truth!" I begged, twisting my tail. "Do I have a bad case of Blue Spot Disease?"

"No, nothing that serious. You're as healthy as 𝔉𝔯𝔢𝔰𝔥 𝔖𝔥𝔞𝔯𝔭 𝔠𝔥𝔢𝔡𝔡𝔞𝔯!" He winked and whispered, "Mr. Stilton, you've got . . . **A BAD CRUSH**!"

Hmmm . . . tongue-tied!

Hee, hee, hee!

WHAT A
FABUMOUSE TEAM!

Grandfather William stared at me over the top of his **glasses** and exclaimed, "A crush? How **SILLY**! Geronimo, don't you dare make me look bad in front of my friend. Get your tail in gear! For now, I'll leave you in charge — but if you don't **shape up**, I'll take over! Understand?"

Get your tail in gear!

I **PROMISED** my grandfather I'd do my very best. Chattering cheddar, what else could I say? As soon as he and Professor Brainymouse left, I was ready to get to work. There

was so much to do, but I couldn't let it ruffle my fur!

My entire **STAFF** and all my **FRiENDS** wanted to help. First, I noted every mouse's age and skill. Then Patty Plumprat helped me organize everything that needed to be done. Soon, every rodent had been given a specific task.

WHAT A FABUMOUSE TEAM!

Trap, Thea, Benjamin, and Bugsy Wugsy offered to come with me to Professor Brainymouse's lab and see how the research was going. Thea was in charge of taking **PhOtOS**, Benjamin and Busgy were writing a **BLOG** to keep our readers informed about the progress, and Trap — well, Trap kept us all laughing with his **JOKeS**.

Together, we headed to the Academy of

WHAT A FABUMOUSE TEAM!

Trap kept us all laughing with his jokes!

Bruce Hyena suggested some exercises to keep the residents of New Mouse City in shape.

My staff made flyers that explained how to strengthen the body's immune system and avoid infection.

Don't touch!

Uncle Samuel S. Stingysnout wanted to be in charge of raising money to finance the research. Since he's known for his stinginess, I decided that Aunt Sweetfur (the most generous mouse in my family) should work with him. Wild Willie and 00K, both experts in martial arts, also joined the fund-raising team. They were ready, willing, and able to protect the money we raised!

Tina Spicytail prepared healthy fruit and vegetable drinks for everyone!

Fresh-squeezed drinks, anyone?

Science, New Mouse City's top scientific university. Professor Brainymouse's team was holed up there, working around the clock to find a cure for the strange blue spots. The **CAMPUS** had been recently built in a brand-new neighborhood on the outskirts of New Mouse City. It wasn't even on the map yet, but everyone already called it the **SCIENCE QUARTER**!

The academy had the most modern science laboratories and the biggest science library on Mouse Island. The very best of the best researchers worked and studied there. MOUSERIFIC!

At the campus entrance, a tall, athletic mouse wearing an oversized lab coat greeted us with a bright smile.

"I bet you're Mr. Stilton!" he squeaked. "I'm Richard Curlytail, assistant and researcher. Call me Rick! This way, please. The professor is waiting for you!"

Thea shook his paw. "Nice to meet you, Rick — I'm Thea, and this is Benjamin, Bugsy Wugsy, and Trap."

"Welcome! For SAFETY and SECURITY reasons, please put on these coats." After giving us lab coats, he handed each of us a small card and squeaked, "Here! These are your **ID BADGES**. Keep them on you at all times!"

SERIOUS SECURITY!

Rick led us through some big rooms, courtyards, warehouses, and stairwells until we finally came to Professor Brainymouse's **laboratory**. He made us all walk single file on a YELLOW LINE as a high-tech camera scanned our eyes. Rat-munching rattlesnakes, this was some serious security!

Suddenly, five MECHANICAL ARMS popped out of the ceiling, all

holding huge pairs of tweezers. They plucked a whisker from each of us. Yow! Holey cheese, that hurt!

"Sorry about the WHiSKeRS," Rick apologized. "But it's a necessary precaution! Now the security system will recognize your EYES and your DNA."*

I nodded. "I understand. I've been in some top secret scenarios before!"

"Listen up, everyone!" Rick squeaked. "Professor Brainymouse's lab requires the highest level of SECURITY. Do you understand?" He lowered his VOICE. "The professor has even given this project a special

LABORATORY SAFETY

In science laboratories, it is very important to follow strict guidelines. These guidelines are for everyone's safety and protection. Lab coats, gloves, goggles, masks, and special hoods are some of the precautions that may be required to avoid exposure to dangerous substances. Laboratories can be subdivided into safety levels; each level is based on the degree of danger it poses and the kind of work under way.

*DNA is the genetic code. It is unique for every living thing.

code name: the Cheese Experiment. That way, other mice won't know what he and his team are working on!"

Once we were all suited up, Rick entered the access code on a **keypad**, and the door to the laboratory opened. He escorted us into the lab, where Professor Brainymouse waved in welcome.

"Welcome to the Cheese Experiment!" he whispered with a wink. "Let me show you around. But please, be very quiet. It's

Professor
Paws von
Volt

Dewey von
Volt

Rick
Curlytail

Wanda
McSlice

Professor Paws von Volt and his nephew Dewey are inventors and scientists. They specialize in time travel!

Rick Curlytail is a brilliant biologist. Wanda McSlice is a bit of a mystery mouse, but she's very smart and capable.

important not to distract the researchers! They're working on very complicated experiments, and they need to keep their snouts down and FOCUS."

He turned to me. "Mr. Stilton, be sure to take good notes. Your grandfather asked me to keep an eye on you! It's important that your readers are *well-informed*."

"Of course," I quickly answered. "I respect my readers!"

| Dr. Swisswhiskers | Professor Astrofur | Vivian von Volt | Dr. Bitmouse, aka Doc |

Dr. Swisswhiskers is a scientist specializing in warts and spots. Astrofur is a great professor!

Vivian von Volt is a philosopher and an expert in bioethics. Doc is unique — brilliant, funny, and as sharp as good cheddar!

I pulled out a **notebook** and began to scribble. First, I wrote down the name and special skills of each researcher.

I spotted Professor Paws von Volt and his nephew **DEWEY**, along with Vivian von Volt, Professor Astrofur, and Dr. Swisswhiskers.

There were other young researchers in the lab, too, including a striking rodent with platinum **blond** fur and icy-blue **EYES** whom I had never seen before. Her name was Wanda McSlice, and she was a biotechnologist with a scholarship paid by a company named **Cheese, Inc.**

And, naturally, **DOC** was there, too.

FORMING A RESEARCH TEAM
A research team can be made up of researchers specializing in various areas. This is helpful because there are often many different kinds of problems to solve! There may be biologists, physicists, chemists, and doctors all on one team. Even philosophers and experts in bioethics can be part of the team!

SQUEAK! MY TAIL TREMBLED, AND MY FUR STOOD ON END!

I was so excited that when I walked past her, I TRIPPED on the leg of a stool. I spun on my paws, did a double flip, landed flat on my belly, and smacked my snout on the floor! **Bang!**

GOOD NEWS AND BAD NEWS

All the researchers turned to look at me, and I **blushed** from the ends of my ears to the tip of my tail.

"**Shhh!** Geronimo, couldn't you stay on your paws for once?" Thea scolded me.

Trap **FLICKED** my ear with a grin. "Try not to be such a cheesebrain, Cuz!"

Rotten rats' teeth!

Just then **WANDA MCSLICE** jumped to her paws and **screeched**, "**Rotten** rats' **TEETH**! I can't work with all this noise!"

She stormed out, **SLAMMING** the door behind her. She certainly had her tail in a twist!

"She's a little edgy," Rick explained, "but she's the best in her field."

Doc gave him a wry look as she walked over and **pinched** me on the cheek.

"Here's my little cheese puff — I heard you coming! It was the familiar **smack** on the floor that gave you away!"

Cheese niblets, how **embarrassing**! "I—I—I didn't trip!" I **stammered**. "I—I wanted to . . . um . . . see if the floor was clean!"

I was a **mess**! Luckily, the professor stepped in and asked us to follow

Here's my little cheese puff!

him to the conference room for an **important** announcement.

Professor Brainymouse sat down behind a large desk, cleared his throat, and said, "Dear colleagues, I have **GOOD** news and **bad** news. Which do you want to hear first?"

"The **GOOD** news!" we all exclaimed.

The professor nodded grimly. "The **GOOD NEWS** is that I discovered the name of this mysterious Blue Spot Disease while I was looking through a very old book. The disease is called **RODENTIA SPOTILITIS**!" He looked at me. "Did you get that, Geronimo?"

"Yes!" I said, my pen flying across the page. "So what's the bad news?"

"The **bad news** is that there's no cure — so it's up to us to find one. Rick will give you all the research protocol!* **GOOD LUCK!**"

The scientists scampered out of the room.

*Research protocol is a detailed description of phases and procedures that every researcher must follow carefully.

Rodentia Spotilitis

What It Is: A very rare disease, described hundreds of years ago in an ancient document titled "The Mysterious Blue Spot Disease." Now the condition is better known as rodentia spotilitis.

Symptoms: Blue spots all over the body — especially on the snout!

How It Evolves: If not addressed, it causes rigidity of the tail. If left untreated for too long, it can even cause the tail to fall off!

Cause: Unknown!

Cure: Unknown!

Current Plan: Analyze the blue spots; find the cause of the disease; find the cure.

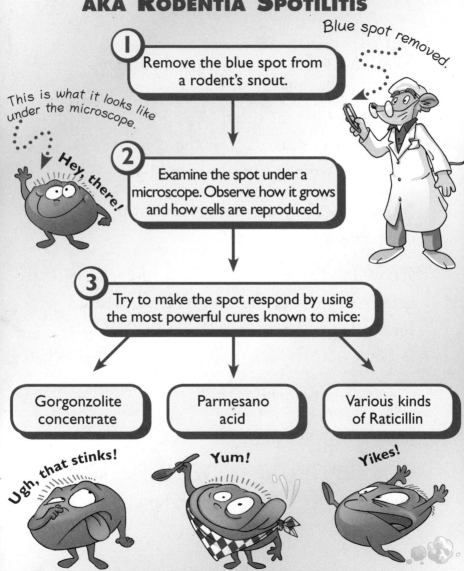

I sat there reviewing my notes and minding my own business when — jumping Jack cheese! A cactus plant pricked me!

"**YOW!**" I squeaked, leaping to my paws.

"Pssst, Geronimo!" the plant whispered. "It's me, Hercule! Did you like my little PRANK?"

I sighed. "No, I didn't! My tail is full of THORNS!"

"Well, it's time to get your tail in gear. From this moment on, I want you to keep an **EYE** on the researchers — don't let them out of your sight for a second! Because they are working

day and night, YOU have to stay awake day and night."

Thundering cat tails! "What if I have to go to the BATHROOM, or if I feel SLEEPY, or if I get hungry?" I protested.

"Geronimo, this is important!" Hercule squeaked. "If you're hungry, have some banana candies. They'll give you energy!" He shoved a pawful of the candies into my mouth.

YUCK!

Yuck!

Eyes Open Day and Night!

From then on, I kept my eyes wide open DAY and NIGHT, just like Hercule instructed.

Professor Brainymouse and his scientists worked around the clock. They worked every second of the day and — **squeak!** — every second of the night, too. They would have forgotten to eat if Tina hadn't come by every day with a pan full of triple-cheese LASAGNA to keep us all going!

The first day went pretty well. The second day, I started seeing stars. The third day, I had raccoon EYES. The fourth day, I looked like a zombie. By the fifth day, I was an enormouse mess!

But the researchers were so engrossed in the Cheese Experiment, they **never seemed to get tired**! That was one tough team of mice!

That night, Wanda McSlice and Doc worked side by side in the **LAB**. They didn't look the least bit tired — not a single drooping whisker between them!

I tried to keep my **EYES** open, but I was getting soooooo sleepy. I tried drinking **fifteen cups** of tea to keep myself awake, but they didn't help at all! Cheese niblets!

I'm feeling fine!

What a headache!

Ughhhhh!

DAY 1

DAY 2

DAY 3

EVERYTHING'S OKAY!

I'M SEEING STARS!

RACCOON EYES

In the dead of night, *Professor Brainymouse* came to check on how the work was going. He even brought me the ancient **BOOK** that talked about Blue Spot Disease.

"I think you'll like it, Geronimo. It's fascinating! I know you have a passion for old books."

Just then Doc squeaked, "Professor Brainymouse, I just made a **mouserific discovery**!"

The professor and Doc scurried into a

Argh!

Squeak!

Triple-cheese lasagna?

DAY 4

DAY 5

I LOOKED LIKE A ZOMBIE!

I WAS AN ENORMOUSE MESS!

corner to talk. Every so often, I could hear the professor cry out:

"FABUMOUSE! AMAZING! MOUSETASTIC!"

For a second, it seemed like Wanda McSlice was trying to eavesdrop on their conversation, but it was probably just my imagination. After all, she was on their team. Why would she need to eavesdrop?

With a shrug, I began flipping through the old book. Cheese and crackers — for a while, I **forgot** how tired I was! The book really was fabumouse. It described the **symptoms** of Blue Spot Disease and explained how it had spread many, many, many years ago. But it didn't say anything about a cause or a possible cure.

As I read, I noticed that some pages were **MISSING**. It looked like pages had been torn

from the book. **HOW STRANGE!**
But then again, the book was incredibly old.
The pages may have just **fallen** out over
time . . . right?

As I thought about it, I felt my
eyelids growing **heavier** . . . and
heavier . . . and **heavier**.
Then, without realizing it, I fell fast asleep!

A TOTAL, ABSOLUTE, DOWNRIGHT DISASTER!

When I finally woke up, I was **TIED** to the swivel chair like a mummy. Slimy Swiss cheese! A voice was **squeaking** urgently in my ear. "Wake up!"

I slowly opened my eyes. Standing in front of me was . . . Hercule! **PHEW!**

He untied me. Then, with his paws on his hips and a stern expression on his snout, he said, "Geronimo! What happened? Didn't I tell you to keep your **EYES** open? I have to go, but meet me at the Cheese, Inc. factory in an hour. There's definitely something *funny* going on!"

I finally looked around and noticed that

the entire laboratory was in **shambles**: upside-down test tubes, broken equipment, flooded floors . . .

It was a total, absolute, downright disaster!

And in one corner, also tied up like a mummy, was Doc. She had a **HUGE LUMP** on her head and was completely unconscious. Whiskers wobbling, I scurried over to free her.

When I reached her, she opened her eyes and said, "My hero! Maybe you're not a cHeeSebRaiN after all!"

My snout turned red. "Hero?" I tried to focus. "What happened? Who clunked you on the head? Did you see anyone?"

"Unfortunately, I didn't see a thing!" she squeaked. "I had just finished telling the professor that I had found a possible CURE for RODENTIA SPOTILITIS. When he left, I turned back to my work. A second later, I felt a THUMP and blacked out . . ."

Wait one whisker-licking minute — Wanda McSlice had disappeared! HOW STRANGE! Without wasting another moment, I set off the alarm.

WOOWOOOWOOOOOOOOOoo
oooooooooooooooooo
ooo!

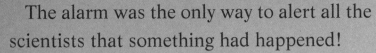

The alarm was the only way to alert all the scientists that something had happened! Professor Brainymouse was the **first** to arrive. "What's going on?" he squeaked urgently. "A fire? A flood? A gas leak?"

"A total, absolute, downright disaster!"

I cried.

What happened?

We're coming!

Soon, all the rodents on **CAMPUS** gathered in the emergency meeting place — the courtyard. The only one **MISSING** was Wanda McSlice. **HOW STRANGE!**

Benjamin, Bugsy Wugsy, and Thea were there. I gave them each a reassuring **HUG**. "Don't get your tails in a twist! Everything's under control . . . almost."

Thea and I helped the professor inspect the laboratories. Unfortunately, everything was destroyed: the microscopes, the computers, the notes!

It was a total, absolute, downright disaster!

Rats — it was going to be impossible to move ahead with the Cheese Experiment!

Only someone truly **EVIL** could have destroyed all the work that so many rodents' tails depended on. (We rodents are very protective of our tails!)

At that moment, I felt a tug on my jacket. It was Benjamin and Bugsy.

"Uncle G, we have an idea," Benjamin said.

"Professor Brainymouse and his team could use the labs at our school!" Bugsy exclaimed. "Think about it: They're brand-new, and they have cutting-edge **COMPUTERS** and microscopes, too!"

HOLEY CHEESE! It was a truly fabumouse idea!

I hugged them both. "Mousetastic thinking — I'm proud of you! Maybe there's still hope for a cure . . ."

Mousetastic thinking!

Woo-hoo!

Hooray!

WANT A BANANA?

Quick as a mouse on a cheese hunt, I called the school principal and New Mouse City's mayor to get permission to use the school **LABORATORIES**.

Professor Brainymouse and his colleagues headed for the school to resume their research. In the meantime, I scurried to meet Hercule at the Cheese, Inc. factory. I ducked behind a **BANANA PLANT** and peeked at the factory — but as I did, the plant **SPOKE**!

"Pssssssst! Hey, Geronimo, want a banana?"

ACK! It was Hercule again!

He signaled for me to be **quiet**. Then he reached into the pocket of his yellow trench coat and pulled out a pair of powerful

binoculars and a strange listening device he had invented to hear distant conversations. He gave them to me and whispered, "Here, Geronimo. Something **SUSPICIOUS** is happening down there, or my name isn't Hercule Poirat!"

I put on the headphones and pointed the **BINOCULARS** toward

I see them!

an open window on the first floor. **Double-twisted rat tails!** I couldn't believe my eyes . . .

In a room on the first floor of the **Cheese, Inc.** factory, I spotted none other than Sally Ratmousen and . . . Wanda McSlice!

In Wanda's paws, I could see the **SCIENTISTS'** notes and a test tube full of liquid. Rancid ricotta! I turned on my headphones and listened carefully.

"**Good job!**" Sally said. "You were right to destroy the Cheese Experiment. Doc was about to discover the **CURE** for

SALLY RATMOUSEN

Wanda McSlice

rodentia spotilitis — but we need to keep it to ourselves! With it, we can ransom all the infected mice. They'll have to give us an enormouse **pile of gold** or . . . *good-bye, tails!*"

Wanda McSlice squeaked, "Yes, but don't forget it was **my** idea to spread rodentia spotilitis throughout the city. I was the one who found the description of the disease in that ancient library book. I was the one to infiltrate the labs. I was the one to stop Professor Brainymouse's team!"

Sally squeaked, "How dare you! This is **my** factory! I built it, I prepared the concentrate to spread the rodentia spotilitis, and I had my airplanes spray it across the city! It was all me!"

Rotten rats' teeth! What horrible rodents! We had to **STOP** them — and fast!

Without thinking twice, Hercule and I ran to the building, LEAPED through the window, and bounded into the room.

Hercule bellowed fiercely,

"Hercuuuule Poiraaaat is heeeere!"

Then he added, "We got you!"
But Sally and Wanda burst out laughing.

"Ha, ha, ha! Try to stop us, cheesebrains!" Sally sneered. "Rodentia spotilitis is everywhere, and we're the only ones with the cure. Either we get a **SACK** of gold, or you can say good-bye to your **TAILS**!"

LET'S TEACH THOSE RATS A LESSON!

Whiskers trembling with anger, I squeaked, "Shame on you, Sally! And Dr. McSlice, you should be **ASHAMED**, too — a scientist should never behave like this!"

"Actually, I'm not a **scientist**," she squeaked with a sly smile. "I'm not even Wanda McSlice!"

She pulled off her wig and top layer of clothing. Holey cheese — it was the SHADOW!

"And I'm not Sally!" the other rodent added, tearing off her disguise, too — **it was the nefarious Sleezer**!

Before Hercule and I could even squeak, the two thieves jumped out the window,

THEIR TRUE IDENTITIES!

First Name: The Shadow
Last Name: Ratmousen
Who She Is: Sally Ratmousen's cousin
Profession: The most notorious thief in New Mouse City! She's willing to do anything to get rich.
Unusual Characteristics: She's known for her clever disguises. She uses a different disguise for every job!

First Name: Sleezer
Last Name: No one knows
Who He Is: A true mystery — no one is sure who he is!
Profession: The most evil, troublemaking rodent on all of Mouse Island
Unusual Characteristics: He always wears a dark trench coat and a large-brimmed hat to hide his snout.

shouting, "Remember! We want a **STACK OF CASH** or **GOOD-BYE, TAILS**! We'll be contacting the mayor soon!"

We **CHASED** them as *FAST* as our paws would carry us. We were closing in when a helicopter appeared out of nowhere and lowered a rope. Sleezer and the **SHADOW** quickly grabbed on.

As they flew away, they **CRIED**, *"Try catching us now, cheddarheads!"*

Suddenly, we heard a **NOISE** in the room we had just left. It seemed to be coming from inside a cabinet. We flung the cabinet door open — and found **Sally Ratmousen** inside!

"It's about time!" she squeaked with a sigh. "Thank you, Geronimo! Wanda McSlice — I mean, the Shadow — locked me in here after she tricked me into **funding** her research!"

"I'm so happy you're not working with

It's Sally!

that awful **SEWER RAT**, Sally —" I began.

But Sally interrupted me. "I am, and will always be, your **ENEMY**! This is just a short truce, for the **GOOD** of all mice. Then we'll go back to being enemies, just like before!"

I shook her paw. "You're one of my competitors, but you will never be an enemy! But fine. **TRUCE!**"

Hercule reached into his trench coat and pulled out a tray holding *three glasses* of banana smoothie.

"How about we toast to it?" he squeaked.

As we toasted, I noticed that the Shadow had dropped TWO SHEETS OF PAPER . . .

Cheese and crackers — these were the pages torn out of the old rodentia spotilitis

Rodentia spotilitis seems to be related to the blue garlic of Ratzikistan!

I have often observed that patients who contract rodentia spotilitis had come into contact with this species of malodorous garlic. Typically, the patients were farmers, those unloading merchandise, and peasants who had inadvertently ingested a piece.

book! And they contained **enormousely important** information! This could almost certainly help Professor Brainymouse find a cure.

We jumped into Hercule's BANANAMOBILE and zoomed to the school laboratories.

"Faster, Hercule, faster!" Sally urged. "Let's teach those **sewer rats** a lesson they won't forget!"

Faster! Faster!

FRIENDS TOGETHER!
MICE FOREVER!

A few moments later, we pulled up in front of Benjamin and Bugsy Wugsy's school. We hightailed it to the laboratory, frantically waving the two missing pages from the old book on Blue Spot Disease. *Professor Brainymouse* scampered toward us, took the pages in his paws, and stared at them for a long time, MURMURING, "Hmm . . . interesting . . ."

We have the cure!

Without squeaking another word, he closed himself inside the lab with his team.

When he finally came out,

he announced, "Friends, we found the cure for **BLUE SPOT DISEASE** — but it needs to be administered within a few hours or it will be too late!"

"Give it to me!" cried Sally. "I can produce an **enormouse** amount of it in my factory!"

"And I'll use my plane to **SPRAY** it over the city," Thea added.

"And I'll keep morale high with my fabumouse *jokes*!" Trap exclaimed. (I tried not to roll my eyes.)

"I'll get out a news flash about the **CURE**!" I squeaked.

Doc piped up, too. "And I'll take care of organizing a **giant party** to get as many mice as possible in one place!"

We all put our paws together and shouted, "Friends together! Mice forever!"

We scampered off as fast as our paws would take us. With Benjamin and Bugsy's help, I wrote a long **article** for *The Rodent's Gazette* titled "The Cheese Experiment." Our readers needed to know the whole truth

about Blue Spot Disease, not to mention Sleezer and the Shadow's blackmail plans!

Once my article was finished and sent to the printer, I remembered that I had barely closed my eyes in days.

I was sleepier than a marathon mouse!

I suddenly felt my eyelids become heavier, and heavier, and **heavier**! I spotted Thea flying over the city in her plane before I fell asleep with a thump.

ZZZZZZZZZ!

When I woke up, Hercule's snout was right in my face. Standing next to him were Thea, Trap, Benjamin, Bugsy Wugsy, and *Professor Brainymouse* — all staring at me with worried looks on their snouts.

HOW STRANGE!

I touched my face and — **cheese niblets!** — felt a huge bump on the tip

of my snout. "Nooooo! A blue spot!"

I almost fainted from fright, but Trap burst out laughing.

"You're such a cheesebrain, Cousin!" he said. "Did you like my little joke? It's just a **fake spot** — the rodentia spotilitis has been cured!"

It was a **HORRIBLE JOKE**, but I was

What's that, Geronimo?

A spot?

Ha, ha, ha!

What's the matter, Uncle G?

so relieved that I couldn't stay angry. I burst out laughing.

"Thundering cat tails — let's party!"

And so the Cheese Experiment came to an end with a bit of a scare, a laugh, and a party with good friends. It was a fabumouse adventure — but we never would have discovered the cure if we hadn't

worked together. After all, every problem has a solution — and together, we can find it!

So long until my next adventure!

Your friend,

Geronimo Stilton

Woo-hoo!

Good job!

Congrats!

Be sure to read all my fabumouse adventures!

#1 Lost Treasure of the Emerald Eye

#2 The Curse of the Cheese Pyramid

#3 Cat and Mouse in a Haunted House

#4 I'm Too Fond of My Fur!

#5 Four Mice Deep in the Jungle

#6 Paws Off, Cheddarface!

#7 Red Pizzas for a Blue Count

#8 Attack of the Bandit Cats

#9 A Fabumouse Vacation for Geronimo

#10 All Because of a Cup of Coffee

#11 It's Halloween, You 'Fraidy Mouse!

#12 Merry Christmas, Geronimo!

#13 The Phantom of the Subway

#14 The Temple of the Ruby of Fire

#15 The Mona Mousa Code

#16 A Cheese-Colored Camper

#17 Watch Your Whiskers, Stilton!

#18 Shipwreck on the Pirate Islands

#19 My Name Is Stilton, Geronimo Stilton

#20 Surf's Up, Geronimo!

#21 The Wild, Wild West

#22 The Secret of Cacklefur Castle

A Christmas Tale

#23 Valentine's Day Disaster

#24 Field Trip to Niagara Falls

#25 The Search for Sunken Treasure

#26 The Mummy with No Name

#27 The Christmas Toy Factory

#28 Wedding Crasher

#29 Down and Out Down Under

#30 The Mouse Island Marathon

#31 The Mysterious Cheese Thief

Christmas Catastrophe

#32 Valley of the Giant Skeletons

#33 Geronimo and the Gold Medal Mystery

#34 Geronimo Stilton, Secret Agent

#35 A Very Merry Christmas

#36 Geronimo's Valentine

#37 The Race Across America

#38 A Fabumouse School Adventure

#39 Singing Sensation

#40 The Karate Mouse

#41 Mighty Mount Kilimanjaro

#42 The Peculiar Pumpkin Thief

#43 I'm Not a Supermouse!

#44 The Giant
Diamond Robbery

#45 Save the White
Whale!

#46 The Haunted
Castle

#47 Run for the Hills,
Geronimo!

#48 The Mystery in
Venice

#49 The Way of
the Samurai

#50 This Hotel Is
Haunted!

#51 The Enormouse
Pearl Heist

#52 Mouse in Space!

#53 Rumble in
the Jungle

#54 Get into Gear,
Stilton!

#55 The Golden
Statue Plot

#56 Flight of the
Red Bandit

The Hunt for the
Golden Book

#57 The Stinky
Cheese Vacation

#58 The Super
Chef Contest

#59 Welcome to
Moldy Manor

The Hunt for the
Curious Cheese

#60 The Treasure of
Easter Island

#61 Mouse House
Hunter

#62 Mouse
Overboard!

The Hunt for the
Secret Papyrus

#63 The Cheese
Experiment

Up next!

#64 Magical Mission

MEET
Geronimo Stiltonord

He is a mouseking — the Geronimo Stilton of the ancient far north! He lives with his brawny and brave clan in the village of Mouseborg. From sailing frozen waters to facing fiery dragons, every day is an adventure for the micekings!

#1 Attack of the Dragons

#2 The Famouse Fjord Race

#3 Pull the Dragon's Tooth!

Thea Stilton and the Dragon's Code

Thea Stilton and the Mountain of Fire

Thea Stilton and the Ghost of the Shipwreck

Thea Stilton and the Secret City

Thea Stilton and the Mystery in Paris

Thea Stilton and the Cherry Blossom Adventure

Thea Stilton and the Star Castaways

Thea Stilton: Big Trouble in the Big Apple

Thea Stilton and the Ice Treasure

Thea Stilton and the Secret of the Old Castle

Thea Stilton and the Blue Scarab Hunt

Thea Stilton and the Prince's Emerald

Thea Stilton and the Mystery on the Orient Express

Thea Stilton and the Dancing Shadows

Thea Stilton and the Legend of the Fire Flowers

Thea Stilton and the Spanish Dance Mission

Thea Stilton and the Journey to the Lion's Den

Thea Stilton and the Great Tulip Heist

Thea Stilton and the Chocolate Sabotage

Thea Stilton and the Missing Myth

Thea Stilton and the Lost Letters

Thea Stilton and the Tropical Treasure

Thea Stilton and the Hollywood Hoax

Thea Stilton and the Madagascar Madness

Don't miss any of my very special editions!

THE KINGDOM OF FANTASY

THE QUEST FOR PARADISE:
THE RETURN TO THE KINGDOM OF FANTASY

THE AMAZING VOYAGE:
THE THIRD ADVENTURE IN THE KINGDOM OF FANTASY

THE DRAGON PROPHECY:
THE FOURTH ADVENTURE IN THE KINGDOM OF FANTASY

THE VOLCANO OF FIRE:
THE FIFTH ADVENTURE IN THE KINGDOM OF FANTASY

THE SEARCH FOR TREASURE:
THE SIXTH ADVENTURE IN THE KINGDOM OF FANTASY

THE ENCHANTED CHARMS:
THE SEVENTH ADVENTURE IN THE KINGDOM OF FANTASY

THE PHOENIX OF DESTINY:
AN EPIC KINGDOM OF FANTASY ADVENTURE

THE HOUR OF MAGIC:
THE EIGHTH ADVENTURE IN THE KINGDOM OF FANTASY

THE WIZARD'S WAND:
THE NINTH ADVENTURE IN THE KINGDOM OF FANTASY

THE JOURNEY THROUGH TIME

BACK IN TIME:
THE SECOND JOURNEY THROUGH TIME

THE RACE AGAINST TIME:
THE THIRD JOURNEY THROUGH TIME

MEET GERONIMO STILTONIX

He is a spacemouse — the Geronimo Stilton of a parallel universe! He is captain of the spaceship *MouseStar 1*. While flying through the cosmos, he visits distant planets and meets crazy aliens. His adventures are out of this world!

#1 Alien Escape

#2 You're Mine, Captain!

#3 Ice Planet Adventure

#4 The Galactic Goal

#5 Rescue Rebellion

#6 The Underwater Planet

#7 Beware! Space Junk!

#8 Away in a Star Sled

Meet
GERONIMO STILTONOOT

He is a cavemouse — Geronimo Stilton's ancient ancestor! He runs the stone newspaper in the prehistoric village of Old Mouse City. From dealing with dinosaurs to dodging meteorites, his life in the Stone Age is full of adventure!

#1 The Stone of Fire

#2 Watch Your Tail!

#3 Help, I'm in Hot Lava!

#4 The Fast and the Frozen

#5 The Great Mouse Race

#6 Don't Wake the Dinosaur!

#7 I'm a Scaredy-Mouse!

#8 Surfing for Secrets

#9 Get the Scoop, Geronimo!

#10 My Autosaurus Will Win!

#11 Sea Monster Surprise

#12 Paws off the Pearl!

ABOUT THE AUTHOR

Born in New Mouse City, Mouse Island, **GERONIMO STILTON** is Rattus Emeritus of Mousomorphic Literature and of Neo-Ratonic Comparative Philosophy. For the past twenty years, he has been running *The Rodent's Gazette*, New Mouse City's most widely read daily newspaper.

Stilton was awarded the Ratitzer Prize for his scoops on *The Curse of the Cheese Pyramid* and *The Search for Sunken Treasure*. He has also received the Andersen 2000 Prize for Personality of the Year. One of his bestsellers won the 2002 eBook Award for world's best ratlings' electronic book. His works have been published all over the globe.

In his spare time, Mr. Stilton collects antique cheese rinds and plays golf. But what he most enjoys is telling stories to his nephew Benjamin.

1. Main entrance
2. Printing presses (where the books and newspaper are printed)
3. Accounts department
4. Editorial room (where the editors, illustrators, and designers work)
5. Geronimo Stilton's office
6. Helicopter landing pad

THE RODENT'S GAZETTE

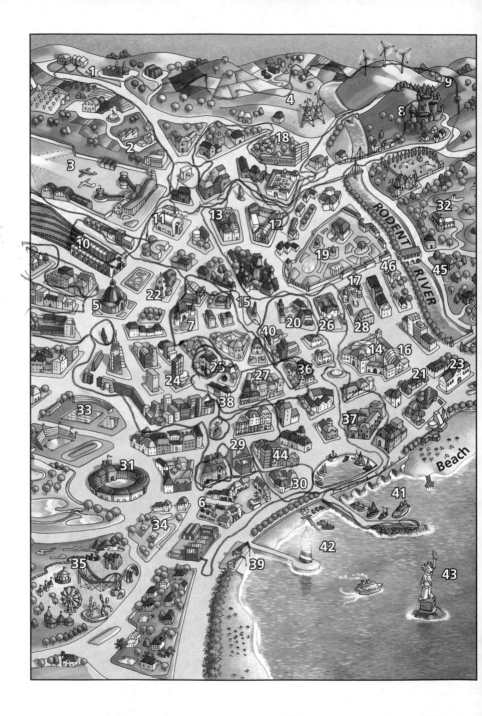

Map of New Mouse City

1. Industrial Zone
2. Cheese Factories
3. Angorat International Airport
4. WRAT Radio and Television Station
5. Cheese Market
6. Fish Market
7. Town Hall
8. Snotnose Castle
9. The Seven Hills of Mouse Island
10. Mouse Central Station
11. Trade Center
12. Movie Theater
13. Gym
14. Catnegie Hall
15. Singing Stone Plaza
16. The Gouda Theater
17. Grand Hotel
18. Mouse General Hospital
19. Botanical Gardens
20. Cheap Junk for Less (Trap's store)
21. Aunt Sweetfur and Benjamin's House
22. Museum of Modern Art
23. University and Library
24. *The Daily Rat*
25. *The Rodent's Gazette*
26. Trap's House
27. Fashion District
28. The Mouse House Restaurant
29. Environmental Protection Center
30. Harbor Office
31. Mousidon Square Garden
32. Golf Course
33. Swimming Pool
34. Tennis Courts
35. Curlyfur Island Amusement Park
36. Geronimo's House
37. Historic District
38. Public Library
39. Shipyard
40. Thea's House
41. New Mouse Harbor
42. Luna Lighthouse
43. The Statue of Liberty
44. Hercule Poirat's Office
45. Petunia Pretty Paws's House
46. Grandfather William's House

Map of Mouse Island

Dear mouse friends,
Thanks for reading, and farewell
till the next book.
It'll be another whisker-licking-good
adventure, and that's a promise!

Geronimo Stilton